About the Author

E. Savoy lives out a lavished fairy tale in her own head while walking endless circles around her children's favorite park beneath a North Dakotan sun. Having sojourned physical realms like a gypsy, Epae has instead been graced to root within unseen, unsung, and unheard realms of fantasy and faith… where she grows. Her hope is that every reader finds their own heartbeat, seen and heard between the lines.

SUITORS, SKELETONS,
& THE
SILENT PRINCESS

E. SAVOY

SUITORS, SKELETONS, & THE SILENT PRINCESS

Vanguard Press

VANGUARD PAPERBACK

© Copyright 2023
E. Savoy

The right of E. Savoy to be identified as author of
this work has been asserted by her in accordance with the
Copyright, Designs and Patents Act 1988.

All Rights Reserved

No reproduction, copy or transmission of this publication
may be made without written permission.
No paragraph of this publication may be reproduced,
copied or transmitted save with the written permission of the
publisher, or in accordance with the provisions
of the Copyright Act 1956 (as amended).

Any person who commits any unauthorised act in relation to
this publication may be liable to criminal
prosecution and civil claims for damages.

A CIP catalogue record for this title is
available from the British Library.

ISBN 978-1-80016-823-7

*Vanguard Press is an imprint of
Pegasus Elliot Mackenzie Publishers Ltd.*
www.pegasuspublishers.com

This is a work of fiction. Names, characters, businesses, places,
events and incidents are either the products of the author's imagination or
used in a fictitious manner. Any resemblance to actual persons, living or
dead, or actual events is purely coincidental.

First Published in 2022

**Vanguard Press
Sheraton House Castle Park
Cambridge England**

Printed & Bound in Great Britain

Dedication

Dedicated to my children, who wanted another princess story…

To every wandering suitor…

And every silent princess.

Acknowledgements

Based on a Turkish fairy tale
The Silent Princess
as compiled by Andrew Lang in
The Olive Fairy Book.

"Like apples of gold in settings of silver, is a word spoken at the proper time."

— Proverbs 25:11, The Holy Bible

Chapter One

Afternoon tea with the sultana, every third day of the week, was nectar to little Calah's eager heart. In preparation, her feet rushed around in a whirlwind that somehow left things better in the aftermath of her spinning. She moved the giant dollhouse to the center of her bedroom, where it looked largest, and set everything in order in that house first — setting out teensy china cups and saucers, adorned with tinier hand-drawn pink roses, petite cloth napkins, and settling all of the dear little bear people around their small table inside. Then, she took to managing her own larger table, the table she and the sultana, her mother, would share.

Lili brought in the hot tea and helped the child set out the delicate, vintage, china teacups and saucers with pink roses that matched the miniature set, while Calah continued brightening the rest of the room — opening curtains, nesting her dolls and stuffings together in neat groups of three, and lightening the hearts of all the staff who saw her so devotedly at work.

Everyone agreed that this was the finest moment of every week on account of the princess's quietness and the sultana's enjoyment of the event. Just before the scene was set perfectly today, however, the trim girl was summoned to her mother's side — to her mother's side in her grandmother's room, to her grandmother's room in the yellow marble castle, in the yellow marble castle that sat in the Golden Valley.

"Come in, Calah," her mother beckoned softly from the grandmother's bedside.

"Mama...," Calah sprinted across the floor to escape the shadows of the room, "it's tea time."

Calah clasped her mother's slender fingers in her perfectly miniatured ones, but her eyes never left the crumpled frame and hollowed eyes of her grandmother. The room was darkly lit and caused the bedridden figure to wane in the shadows where everything smelled like death and looked like defeat.

"Grandmama is very sick. I'm sorry to miss your tea today, Calah."

The little cup of Calah's expectations tripped over her heartbeat and spilled nectar all over the floor of her bones, where it hardened like sap. But hope deferred was in a staring match with death, and the child had her druthers between them.

"Yes, Mama."

"Run along now," sultana replied. The corners of her mouth pulled the weight of her words.

"Yes, Mama."

Little Calah did not like the look of anything in that room. Not even her own mother looked right there, so she did not argue the matter further; but beneath the chill of her growing avoidance of her grandmother's room, she left an untidy gap for bitterness and its perfidious simmer, not yet understanding that the shadows she hated so very much always begin in the light of a justified cause — and they were beginning to shade her own thoughts now.

*

A week of "Grandmama will die soon," passed and Calah had scarcely seen her mother in all that time and, though she tried to amuse herself with her dollies, stuffings, and delicacies, it was her mother's attention that she most desired. Still, she dared not to visit her grandmama unless summoned. Intangible unpleasantries suffocated that room so that she could not bear to go, even to find her adored mother.

When Lili suggested — *and she often did* — that she visit her mother, wherever she may be found, Calah simply replied, "I don't want to" or "Not right now" because the truth was that the little girl didn't have a good reason... only bad feelings.

When came the third day of the next week and Grandmama still had not died, the resilient princess set to work on setting everything in order for afternoon tea with the sultana again because desire and routine are terribly demanding things, especially for a seven-year-old.

The servants and attendants watched inconspicuously from the hall, half bemused and half enchanted by the twirling, humming, tender-footed little girl. They watched her push the giant dollhouse into the middle of the room, as she had done every third day of the week for several years now; they watched her meticulous fingers gently set an entire miniature house in order — as precisely as a hummingbird's beak probing delicate petals for sweet nectar; they watched her smile rise and fall with her chest and lead her feet around the large room. And they all agreed that this was the finest moment of the week on account of the child's quiet cheer and bold hope, though on this particular day such a sight caused the staff to weep.

Didn't the child know that her grandmama was dying? Didn't she know that her mother would not come? Didn't she understand?

But, of course, little Calah did not understand and it was because the staff understood that they wept for her. Good Lili reminded the child that her mother was distracted with care for her own mother, but Calah only continued humming and preparing the table. So, Lili brought in the hot tea and helped her set the larger table as she had always done before.

Then, Calah sat and waited. She waited so long that she nearly forgot why she was waiting, as she folded and refolded the napkins, rubbed the tiny pink roses of her gown between her finger and thumb and admired the delicate folds of each petal and the sage green leaves;

she sipped hot — warm — tepid — cool — tea while waiting, and a late summer breeze drifted in through the balcony doors as the sun poured warm puddles of light into the spacious room.

When bold hope began to abandon the girl, impatient disillusionment set to work and soured every precious thing in the room. Now, when Calah looked around she saw the truth — the truth that the dolls had grown old, the roses were silly, the stuffings were stupid, and afternoon tea with her mother was a childish game. Her mother probably thought it was stupid too; maybe that's why she didn't come...

Little Calah burst from her early childhood skin and pushed the dollhouse over — *CRASH*. Then she threw the precious, heirloom, china teapot and cups from the balcony, sending them to their splintered fates on the jagged rocks below. A few stuffings met with the same fate before the girl fell into her own tears on the floor screaming —

"I hate Grandmama! I hate her!"

Good Lili, who had stood nearby and witnessed the whole unraveling, rushed to her side and comforted the girl, stroking her long, dark, thick hair and making soft shushing sounds. After little Calah was soothed, they both set to work putting the room back in order. The child put Lili under strict orders not to tell her mother what had happened that afternoon and Lili, empathetic towards the child, nodded her agreement that it should be so.

Still, the staff found it impossible to hide the fact that the sultan's grandmother's china rose teapot had been dashed on the rocks outside of the yellow marble castle. When he discovered it, in his anger, he excoriated Calah for her own bad temper and banished her to spend the remainder of the week in her own quarters, which, of course, did nothing to improve her temper. The sultan had not permitted her a chance to explain her misery or why she had thrown the teapot; though he might have guessed why had he been a more interested father; however, he was very busy with diplomatic affairs and did not suffer such outbursts from his own carefully bred daughter.

Now, little Calah had suffered fits of anger before, but this specific punishment, set her tongue on fire and loosened a biting wind from the lungs in her chest that she could not easily put back. She saw now that she was *right* to be angry at her mother, *right* to be angry with her father, and *right* not to visit her grandmama, whose sickness had opened the first trickle that caused the entire waterfall of events against her previously ordered life.

As Calah sat quietly on her plush pillows and pattered around in her fine adornments for several days afterwards, no one could have suspected the windblown fire raging within the girl that needed but a bit of oxygen behind her tongue to spread. When the staff passed by her room, they passed slowly — wondering, pitying, and speculating about the child in their own minds. Lili even tried to play dollies with her once, but the child sat motionless and stared through the woman until she left.

Nonetheless, on the fourth day after the sultan had confined the child to her bedroom, the doctor assured the sultana that the grandmama was surely about to surrender her last breath and Calah was summoned again to her grandmama's side by the sultana.

"Calah." The sultana held her hand out and motioned for the girl to enter the room.

She took her mother's hand, desiring more than anything to be with her again outside of that room but despising every lingering breath of the distorted figure in the bed.

"I wish she would die," leapt out of her heart and plunged right through her lips.

The sultana felt Calah's grip tighten as she said the spiteful words and knew that her daughter meant them. She straightened her slumped back and looked down at the child in a way that brought the girl's gaze up to her mother.

"You have been careless with your words, Calah. This is like a castle falling down upon my own heart," she said, lips trembling. "But you must bear the consequence of such carelessness; therefore, Calah of the Golden Valley, I curse you with the Veil of Silence."

Little Calah's body suddenly shook, her eyes like prey, helpless before the sultana's power. Immediately, a veil appeared over the child's mouth, extending from ear-to-ear on either side and held up by an invisible power. The girl reached up and tried to pull it off, scratching her own face in the process, but material power had not put it there and material power could not release it.

"Mama! Why? — Do you hate me so?" she cried.

The sultana stood and the room dimmed in her shadow. "These are my mother's final moments. We will discuss this later, Calah."

Calah fled the room with all of the haste of a sparrow escaping a crow. Carelessness, however, remained in her, and she never spoke another word to her mother.

Her grandmama died that night.

Chapter Two

Once a month the much-coveted-and-noble pasha took his fine young son to the marketplace, where they would inspect new merchant wares and select a few special items to take home. They might return from their usually joyous trip with any number of delightful things: exotic fruits, a new carpet, toy tin soldiers, an animal-shaped candle, new shoes, a book, or some regal stationery. For the boy, the hunt was as inspiring as the careful selection, though young Ayaz was often ready to make a selection long before the pasha approved, and this day was no different.

Young Ayaz knew the moment he saw the caged and exotic bird that he must have it. Bright green with rosy cheeks, the young parrot delighted the boy with its chatter that resembled their own speech, though the only word known to the bird was "Hello" and it squawked out the two-syllable word repeatedly and — *in the pasha's words* — obnoxiously.

"Please, father; can't we have the bird?"

Young Ayaz tugged at the much-coveted-and-noble pasha's decorated uniform and pointed back to the caged creature still in sight behind them.

His father grunted and shook his head. "No."

Ayaz's smile shriveled.

The pasha tried to lure his boy with several other trinkets saying, "Come. Let's look at the small knives here" and "Oh, this is a fine book" or "Wouldn't these marbles be a nice addition to your collection" — but Ayaz would have none of it.

"I want the bird, papa," he whined.

This request, however, would never be granted by the young boy's father, who despised pets of all kinds; finding the caretaking bond between humans and animals too strange and personal, and believing that it encouraged weakness on the human side. Though the same might be said of having children, the pasha did not see this as the same thing. "No" was his solid reply to the son he hoped to soon train for military service.

Now, young Ayaz was still a boy and not a soldier and no amount of colorful marbles would make up for the injustice he felt about the matter. All of his playmates had pets — dogs, ponies, a snake, or at least a stray cat — and he would never agree with the much-coveted-and-noble pasha's feelings on the matter. When his human playmates were busy, he could have a companion in a pet; when the pasha was entertaining dignitaries, he could have entertainment in a pet; when he tired of pretending to toss his favorite golden ball to a phantom, he could enjoy petting or talking to his pet instead. And he made all of these points to his father too, to no avail.

Upon returning home, the boy tossed the new marbles his father had chosen aside and went to the courtyard to play with his golden ball. At first, still thinking only of his disappointment, he rolled the ball here-and-there half-heartedly, but, when anger had attached its full weight behind disappointment, he sought a larger challenge and began aiming to shoot the ball out of the courtyard window. It was a small arched window beside the iron gate that led out to the town well. Accomplishing the feat, he then had to fetch the ball.

Once outside of the courtyard gates, he saw an old widow coming to the well with an earthen vessel to gather water. Misdirecting his anger, he threw the ball as hard as he could and broke the poor woman's vessel.

Looking regal in his market clothes and knowing that she wouldn't likely touch him because of the much-coveted-and-noble pasha, he stood with triumphant arms crossed. She looked at him, perhaps in shock, and left, but as the boy was still rolling his ball alongside the outside courtyard walls, she returned with a new pitcher; and, again, he threw the golden ball and shattered the earthen vessel.

This time, the old widow glared at the boy, but knowing his father was the much-coveted-and-noble pasha, she held her tongue and left again. Just as young Ayaz was about to open the iron gates and put his ball away, however, she returned a third time with a new pitcher she had purchased in town like the first two.

Again, the boy did as he had done previously and broke the old widow's water vessel.

Being ill-tempered from her many trips to the well and the money she had spent on pitchers, she cursed the boy:

"May you fall in love with The Silent Princess!"

Ayaz laughed. What sort of a thing was that to say? And who was 'The Silent Princess'?

Still, knowing he might not get away with his shameful deeds so easily next time, he put the ball away and retrieved his new marbles to play with for the remainder of the day. And, for a time, the young boy forgot all about the bird and all about the old widow's peculiar words...

*

Lala Lalu leapt aside as the young man, Ayaz, hurled a golden plate across the dining room, barely missing him. The plate split like lightening against the wall.

"Why won't they accept me!"

It was more of a rant than a question, of course, and, had this been the first or even the second time the dear attendant's friend had been refused by a local female, he might have scolded him for such an outburst; however, it was the twenty-fourth time, and Lala Lalu felt the thunder of his friend's pain.

"Lala Lalu, tell me — Am I an octopus with eighteen arms? A dolphin with no nose? Am I like a rat turned inside out? Or a mangy dog with a stork's beak? — Please!" Ayaz slammed both hands down on the other end of the table and hung his head, then added: *"If I am ugly in some unknown way, I beg of you to tell me."*

Lala Lalu's lips pursed into a frown. The much-coveted-and-noble pasha's son had been good to him and provided him with work and an income prior to friendship, and he hated to see him suffer so. The truth was that he did not know why Ayaz was not only refused by these women but, so often, *hastily* refused. It was as much a mystery to him as it was to his friend; nonetheless, he tried to speak in a comforting way.

"There is nothing at all unpleasant about you, Ayaz. Truly, if you lack anything it is only patience."

Ayaz's head shot up.

"Have I not been patient!"

"Yes. No one would deny it… I think endurance is the word I meant," Lala Lalu answered, nervously, because he was a good and honest friend.

The grown Ayaz took a deep breath and nodded. He knew that Lala Lalu had not meant him any harm, but his friend's words brought back to mind the one thing he had tried for several years now to ignore…

He shook his head. How could it be? Was the old widow a witch? Was there truly power in her words: 'May you fall in love with The Silent Princess'? And, if so, who was The Silent Princess?

"Have you ever heard of The Silent Princess?"

Lala Lalu shrugged, grateful to be put into a less heated topic.

"I've never heard of such a princess. Do you know her?"

"No..." Ayaz breathed in deeply. "But I feel like I should."

They said nothing more about the hypothetical princess that day, but the more Ayaz thought about the widow's words, The Silent Princess, and his constant rejection by the local women, the more morose he became with belief that these things were somehow connected. But how was he to chase a myth? And how could a bleak widow's words prove so powerful?

Nevertheless, Lala Lalu could not cheer his friend or coax him out for a hunt or a drink; the pasha could not entice him with duties or accolades of upcoming missions; and he no longer bothered to pursue any of the young, single women in town. One day he fell into bed and refused to be comforted at all by food or drink or company. He thought only of The Silent Princess; but he thought of her despairingly, for he imagined that he would never know her.

The much-coveted-and-noble pasha grew increasingly bewildered over his son's strange malaise and finally begged the young man to reveal the plague invading his mind and body, so Ayaz told him the story of the widow and his golden ball and the frightful words she had spoken over him so long ago. Wanting only for his son to be well, the pasha asked his son what should be done to remedy the situation.

"Shall we buy the old hag another pitcher?" he asked.

"No, no, father. Was she wrong in her words since I broke three pitchers for which she had to pay? If a new pitcher would have sufficed, wouldn't she have asked you for it?"

Ayaz sat up in bed now, rejuvenated by sharing his burden with his father (as he had not shared the story with anyone else until then), and said:

"I must find The Silent Princess, father. You must permit me this great quest or I fear I shall never be rid of the widow's words. Perhaps this quest is how she meant for me to repay her."

Such light flooded Ayaz's beautiful brown eyes upon these words that his father could not find resolve to refuse him. So it was that the pasha agreed to his son's mission to find The Silent Princess, and sent him on his way with Lala Lalu as his friend and guardian, along with two horses, food, and other small provisions.

*

Now, the eager Ayaz's heart had swollen with such good hope in his endeavor that he took no counsel concerning which way to trod, but heartily sang happy tunes atop his handsome horse, permitting the beast to lead them into the forest. Lala Lalu followed on his horse feeling equally content with the leading, since it made his friend so lighthearted and it had been many weeks since he had seen him so cheerful. Besides, they did not know where they were going, so any direction seemed just as well. After a week of rocky nights, dwindling provisions, sores and blisters, however, hope began to trail somewhere behind them, dragging their good moods down with it.

"Where is this my heart has led me?" Ayaz mused aloud.

"I think we're lost," Lala Lalu answered, practically.

Neither men recognized the forest now; they could scarcely distinguish one tree, another rock, or this dusty trail from another. They had both done a reasonable march of traveling under the much-coveted-and-noble pasha's command, but never in such blithe manner with so vague a compass as a bit of heart, a fever of mind, and a widow's words to guide them. Nevertheless, the young, bright men had no intention of surrendering their mission.

Still, Ayaz and Lala Lalu also had no idea yet about how far they would need to travel to find The Silent Princess, so they kept up in this way for another month, exchanging despair and frustration for song and friendly banter, making light of their present discomforts. But the day finally came when singing and longing simply weren't enough to face the very real hardships of the journey, because they had meandered when they should have plotted.

It was on this day that the two men decided to stop near a stream for the day and sharpen sticks to spear some fish to eat. They had not yet seen another soul, village, or hut along the way and each man was weary of trying to keep up the spirits of the other, so they passed most of the day in silence fishing, searching for other edibles to stash away, and washing. It was a much needed rest, though neither could admit so out loud.

Surprise was hardly the word for it when the trapper snuck up on them as they cooked their fish over a nice fire that evening. Ayaz had a sword at the older man's chest within seconds and Lala Lalu held the knife they had used to clean the fish in a defensive position from below, where he sat on an old log still swallowing his mouthful.

The trapper smiled broadly at the two young men but did not flinch. He was covered in bits of pieced-together fur and wore a large belt that dangled with various traps, knives, and nets. How he managed to sneak up on anyone was a question never answered in the young men's minds.

"You've wandered far," he stated, cheerfully.

"Who are you?" asked Ayaz.

"It's *my* woods and fish; who are *you*?"

"I am Ayaz and this is Lala Lalu. We're just passing through," Ayaz replied and put away his sword, realizing that the stranger was only armed with traps and a smile.

The smile never left the trapper's face; it was so broad and eager that Lala Lalu couldn't help but wonder if he was mocking them in some secret way. Nonetheless, being trained to mind his own business and believe the best of others, Lala Lalu said nothing of these feelings and thought the smiler must have been a lonely man in such endless woodlands. Seeming to confirm these suspicions, the trapper scratched his scruffy chin and made a hearty offer:

"We don't get much company out here. If you want a real meal, I have three daughters at home who would be delighted to cook for two young men."

Ayaz and Lala Lalu looked at each other and hastily accepted. Ayaz thought it to be a reasonable gesture of goodwill and understood that it would be a social rudeness to decline the request since they had trespassed upon the man's own territory, and Lala Lalu was hungry for a real meal. The trapper assured them that his home was only a short walk away and that they would soon have their bellies filled with sweet meats and a merry time to ease their way.

Two trapping stories and a bunny trail later, a dear home appeared made from logs and nestled amongst the trees as if the logs had never been felled from the woods but only rearranged there. It was humble but broad enough to keep two guests comfortable and, as predicted by the trapper, his three daughters were soon clanging pots, clutching aprons, and readying food in a pale-faced panic to please the young men who did not mind being pleased.

Being so well fed and pampered by the young women, it was not difficult for the trapper to convince the men to stay another day. He reminded them of the blistered bottoms, backaches, and prior hunger they had already endured, and urged them to take one more day of ease to lighten their feet and brighten their smiles. So, the young men stayed the night comfortably.

Now, Ayaz had never been fawned over by the women in his own town, and these three made such a fuss over him that he was quite tempted to consider them, but they showed no less interest in Lala Lalu, so that he was confused about their intent.

Did they mean to have any man? Would any man suit them just as well?

Despite his prior rejections, Ayaz could not bring himself to feel this way about just *any* woman and, amid the flirting of the following morning, his heart still sought to continue its seeking for The Silent Princess. He did not know, however, that a trap was already set and was soon to be sprung when the eldest daughter, who was refused a kiss by Ayaz, ran to tell her father.

"What's this you mean? Why have you disgraced my daughter?"

The trapper bracketed his thunderous shouting with smiles at both ends, as if there were some unspoken social code to keep up with, *When you shout, be sure to smile and win a friend amid your wiles* — or something. But these foreign traits only made Ayaz nervous.

"She tried to kiss me, and I refused. If that disgraces her, it is *her* disgrace," he replied, flatly.

The girl burst into tears and fled to a bedroom. Her father pinched his scruffy chin and pursed his lips.

"Well," he finally began, "You must forgive girls who want husbands, especially when they live in the woods."

The menfolk nodded, none wanting to entirely upset the other on account of having shared a good time. Nevertheless, the other two daughters did not take long to follow upon the tails of their sister's apron — one pressing against Lala Lalu her desire to be taken and the other caressing Ayaz's lovely black locks with pitiful eyes of longing.

Both men stood, suddenly sobered from the last evening's wine.

"We must go now," Ayaz burst.

"Let's," Lala Lalu agreed.

Tripping over apologies to the ladies, they made a quick exit — into the trapper's arms, at the door.

"What's this?"

"We're on an important mission!" Ayaz hustled out from underneath one of his arms.

"Already stayed too long!" Lala Lalu added, slipping out from the other side.

As they ran, they could hear the girls sobbing over their father who was yelling out at them as they ran —

"Come back! Why can't you take two? They never see young men! Have pity on an old trapper!"

When the men returned to their steeds, they readied them and rode through much of the night to be sure to put a good distance between them and the home of the trapper's daughters. Still, feeling they had wasted much time, they prayed to run across some other forest dweller so that they might learn some directions to The Silent Princess.

"We took too many chances back there, Lala Lalu," Ayaz concluded, yawning with the next morning's light.

"Within the belly bursts sin's fruition. Next time we eat the fish and be glad."

"Agreed."

Chapter Three

Now, as anyone unfortunate enough to be cursed with the Veil of Silence knows, the veil does not inhibit one from speaking; nonetheless, it effectively discourages careless speech after a while. Three years passed, and little Calah stood in front of her dressing mirror on her tenth birthday examining the damages — *a veil three layers thick.* A new layer had been supernaturally crafted and added over her nose and mouth for every careless year, but this was the first year that she began to feel the weight of it pulling against her temples.

"Another veil?" Lili asked, moving gently alongside the girl.

Calah's eyes flooded from unseen and stirred subterranean rivers. Her small hands hung like golden balls at each side, ready to be thrown. Some years the walls held, but not this year: she burst into sobs, unclenched her fists, and threw them around her patient handmaid.

Lili, who had been loved as well as hurt by the dear girl, shushed and embraced her.

"Your mother wants to speak with you about this, Calah."

"I will not!"

The girl screamed the reply into Lili's softly wrapped garment.

"It was her riddle that placed the veil, girl; I don't think it wise to be stubborn."

Calah stopped sobbing but continued to cling to the handmaid who had become her only friend, mother, and confidant since that fateful day and, ergo, also her most mistreated companion.

"I know what she will say," she answered. "She'll say 'As soon as you speak rightly the veil will go away' —That's what she'll say, and I will not hear it."

Lili pushed the child gently to an arm's length and locked eyes.

"If you *know*, why not *do*?"

"She doesn't deserve to be heard!"

Lili's face contorted with tenderness around the muscle of the girl's hard words. The earnestness of her bedazzling hazel eyes almost made the child doubt her own way, though it would be a while yet — *not this year, nor the year after, nor the year after that* — before Calah took her good Lili's words to heart.

"Can a child be led where they do not wish to go?" Lili questioned aloud but drew the little one into another hug. "But I do not know whether you are right about your mother's words, darling. I wish you would ask her."

*

Another fitful and difficult four years passed with Calah's father busy in territorial squabbles and the affairs of men, and her mother distracted with social obligations and the affairs of women, as the little girl grew into a young woman. Every year, for seven years now, the little girl had earned another layer upon her veil and, upon this seventh year, the young woman, feeling resentful and tired, chose never again to speak lest the throbbing pain above her ears increase by the weight of still more veils.

But such vows of will are often untimely-spoken, for not a week had passed after willing such resolve when the sultana died suddenly in the night, and Calah mourned silently because she had not meant to never speak again to her mother — she had only meant it to be for a while. Nevertheless, the passing of her mother was the blood upon the young woman's unspoken contract. Calah meant to teach everyone a lesson — living or dead. The sultana had cursed her to learn to speak rightly, so she would not speak at all. Not even good Lili could put the breath back behind the stubborn woman's tongue.

Naturally, there was only one thing for her father to do at this time and that was to bring in suitors for the princess, but this did not go well. Princes, feeling snubbed by Calah's silence, often left offended and uttered curses against the sultan's kingdom as they left. However, the sultan's reputation was largely saved as each of the suitors suffered untimely deaths the moment they left the yellow marble castle after calling on the princess.

After the first several suitors died, it was rumored that the sultan himself was killing them, but this was not so and his innocence in the matter was eventually proven. This, to the sultan's great relief, turned into his advantage. Word spread throughout the land of a mysterious supernatural force that protected the princess and her father's kingdom and turned the winning of the princess from an anathema into a highly competitive and much envied spectacle — with brothers betting against brothers and enemies daring one another.

Soon after, those far and wide came to seek out 'The Silent Princess', and this brought fame, visitors, and greater wealth to his kingdom. Even the sultan's enemies began to find cause to befriend him, all desiring to hear the stories of the suitors and the skeletons. Indeed, the sultan himself wagered bets here and there for and against certain suitors, but the outcome was always the same: *a silent princess and a dead suitor.*

Perhaps the greatest worldly loss had been that of the famed and magnificent Prince Eratoo, a pretty one from the distant East with great riches and impeccable manners but also enormous pride. Esteemed for his knowledge of the sciences and mystery schools, he had brought the princess a map of the whole earth, beautifully hand drawn by his own noble fingers, and he had read to her from Aesop's fables, though it seemed he had not taken the stories to heart. He had been drawn to The Silent Princess by his vanity alone, for everyone warned him not to go, but he was convinced no other suitor could win such a trophy — thus he reasoned he could not lose.

His skull is the pretty one perfectly blanched by the afternoon sun sitting inside the broken teapot.

A murderous hornet had stung him the moment he left the palace; he swelled until his skin was without wrinkle, perfectly smooth, and died on the marble floor between the colonnades. Where the first few suitors were returned to their countries or buried, rumor, reverence, and caution stood firm and insisted that all subsequent victims be abandoned in a morbid show of superstition they called 'respect'. Prince Eratoo's body was piled with the others on the hill that flanked the west side of the castle, where scavengers took from the body what had not already been pilfered by less superstitious souls, and wild dogs pillaged the rest. A hillside of skulls was all that remained after a while; a brazen and emblazoned forewarning to all who passed or came calling.

Still they came — they came with bears and brushes and ivory clutches, with honey and spices and golden crowns, with diamonds and rubies and sapphires, with golden daggers, marble statues, and ancient fruits — all to persuade The Silent Princess to speak. However, Prince Eratoo, and others like him, were no great loss to the princess, who saw through their charades of kindness and parades of spoiling and words that rang hollow. In being silent for a very long time she had learned better how to listen, and listening had taught her a lot about men.

It was always the same theater. He'd come in like a tender breeze and praise her fortitude against other suitors, her beauty, and her veil. Then, he might spend a few evenings or a week telling her stories of life back home, ending every evening by asking for her hand in marriage and promising to ask again the next night — *'even unto forever* — 'when she did not hastily answer.

Eight days was the longest any had lasted, and it was not unusual for the suitor to explode from the castle by the end of the third day, utterly foiled by her silence. The ones who entered telling jokes about how nice it was for a woman *not* to speak were always the *first* to leave — because to speak or not to speak wasn't really what mattered to them but whether they could control her. When they found they couldn't manipulate the princess with finery, they lost their lacy manner and revealed their true nature. In the beginning, God himself had called Eve a 'helper', after all, not a trophy.

Still, rich or poor, brave or naive, noble or tyrant, Calah lamented that they died just the same, as some seemed more worthy than others. She had no more control over their fates than they did, however, and she could do little more than lament. None, even when beautiful, had been worth the trouble of speech or marriage — *especially if it should mean another veil, another weight, another reminder of her cursedness.* She could not will herself to do it, though she had desired to more than once. The pain of her temples, or maybe her heart, was simply too great for words.

Of course, she thought these things because she had come to believe that her every word was damning and careless. She wondered now whether there was a right or wrong way to speak and whether she could discern the right way at all, therefore, she simply could not will herself to speak even when the suitor seemed worthy.

Chapter Four

Full on the trapper's daughters 'fine meals, and yet nauseated by their own narrow escape of hypothetical horrors, Ayaz and Lala Lalu rode for several days without stopping, dozing here and there and still without direction — knowing what they wanted but not how to get there. When they saw her, both men thought that they were hallucinating, rather than really seeing the breathtaking creature and so rode past her at first.

"Whoa." Ayaz turned his steed around to gawk and wonder, after passing the woman.

It was a vixen, a woman with skin paler than the brightest moon, with waves of hair fierier than the brightest copper glistening beneath the hot sun of their hometown marketplace. She was wrapped in sky blue, head to toe, and a necklace of various crystals hung from her throat tinkling as she gathered wood. Ayaz addressed her first.

"Good day, woman."

Both men stared at the woman and the woman stared back.

Perhaps, thought Lala Lalu, they did not address her correctly.

"Pray, tell us your name, fair lady."

She stood holding the wood, looking more uncomfortable with her task than interested in their pleasantries, shifting the weight between her arms. Ayaz jumped from his black horse and took the chopped wood from the woman.

"Let me help."

Lala Lalu, hoping this wasn't another trap, tied both steeds to a convenient tree and followed his friend, who now followed the woman into the unknown. With silence as their only other companion, the men began to speculate — each to himself — that, perhaps, they had accomplished their mission: *Was this The Silent Princess?*

They followed her so far that the woodlands eventually disappeared from behind them and the full high sun of a far drier landscape soon clawed at their eyes. Nevertheless, the warmth of it was welcome, for they had spent a long time in the woods with nothing but fractals of the giant light upon them. After their eyes had adjusted to the light, they realized that an enormous doorway was before them, etched within towering and gold-dusted bluffs.

The men gave each other a knowing look upon such a sight. *If anyone was The Silent Princess, was it not she?* For the great door certainly suggested the beginnings of a mythical royalty carved within the cliffs. They smiled at one another, and neither man would admit that the little remaining food in their bellies had suddenly turned to ash.

Tucked away neatly, to the right of the pointed crown doors, the tiniest of bells, encased in an arched nook in the wall, was rung by the woman when they arrived. Ayaz and Lala Lalu might have laughed to think that such a small bell would be heard, but they did not have time for such thoughts, for a louder bell rang out clearly, hidden from their view; then a bell louder still after that, somewhere above their heads, until the doors were finally pushed open from within by two smartly dressed giants.

After following the woman inside, the doors were firmly closed behind them and the two young men, feeling that they might have been rather eager again, began to sweat. They had never seen a giant until now and the larger-than-life sighting had dwarfed their confidence as their eyes struggled to adjust to the sudden dimness within — a dimness that swallowed them like a black hole gasping for light.

The giants took up torches and led the small group up some stairs and through another doorway into a larger chamber where a gorgeous fire roared from a blonde brick hearth. A crow cackled at the men from above the hearth — then another and another. In fact, the entire room was lined with large, evil-eyed crows looking down upon them, sitting upon a high shelf that surrounded the room.

Ayaz threw the wood into the fire but did not take his eyes off the crow perched above. Lala Lalu grabbed his arm afterwards and yanked -

"We should go, Ayaz."

Lala Lalu's eyes darted around the room from crow to crow and then back to his friend, but it was too late by then. His friend had just locked eyes with the vixen, who seemed to silently beckon him from across the room with the faintest of smiles dancing across her lips.

She sat upon a luxurious bed of silks and pillows surrounded by silver dishes, all full of dates and raisins. Two silver candlesticks stood on either side of the bed. Neither man had noticed that she had removed her shoes, but the darling sight of her ankles peeking out from beneath her garment was arguably the prettiest thing the weary men had seen in months.

"She is bewitching you!" Lala Lalu warned, keeping his voice low, but Ayaz was already swaying against his restraint and pulling away from his friend. Lala Lalu let go.

Many statues lined the walls of the chamber. Crows with crowns and children holding scepters made up the primary muse of the molded figures, but it was a small section of books along one wall that caught Lala Lalu's attention. As he read each title of every book on the seven shelves, his fears spawned and appeared alive and well before his waking eyes; there was not one book aligned there that did not bear the word 'silent 'or 'silence 'or 'unspoken 'against its spine. Though he knew nothing of The Silent Princess, Lala Lalu felt he could discern enough from a man or woman's book collection — and he had never known a good woman who was also silent. Only the cunning ones.

It was this thought that caused him to look again upon his friend, who had reclined upon the bed with the enchantress, and he found them both fast asleep. To his great dismay, he alone had been left awake in the hot room full of eyes, and he was exceedingly tired from travel.

He yawned — which was just enough laxness to frighten him to stay awake a bit longer, for which he was later very glad. Indeed, he had scarcely sat down in a chair to wait or snooze when a large and gruff looking crow descended and perched upon his shoulder. Lala Lalu startled and winced.

"Sit, friend," the crow hastened, "but do not sleep!"

"You talk," Lala Lalu replied, amazed.

"I'll tell you more than that," the bird said keeping his tones hushed. "I was once a man like your friend!"

The crow's words sliced a nerve and deadened Lala Lalu's tongue but his mind was never sharper as he listened.

"Once she puts them to sleep, she does not lightly let them go again. She lures them into dreams and visions that feel so real one cannot discern reality from dream after only a short while. In the end, she captures them like birds in the other realm, then brings them back here and turns them all to crows."

Lala Lalu looked around the room perched above again. The other crows were nodding with murderous eyes.

"All of them?" Lala Lalu swallowed hard.

"Every last one," answered the crow. "So, do your friend a favor: Wake him up now!"

The crow leapt into the air and ascended again with his fellows.

"And don't say we didn't warn you," he crowed from overhead.

Lala Lalu jumped to his feet which now had more of an urgency than fear holding them up, despite his lack of sleep, and went to shake his friend —

"Ayaz! Ayaz! Ayaz! — Wake up!"

He pulled at his friend's arms, shook his friend's head gently, and lifted his feet, letting them fall like dead weights, but nothing seemed to work.

"What should I do?" Lala Lalu asked the crows, desperate.

"If we had known, would we be here?"

"But surely you know now! Haven't you seen her ways? — There must be something!" Lala Lalu screeched.

The crows were silent for a moment, glancing this way and that with beady eyes, but Lala Lalu waited and his patience was rewarded when another crow addressed him.

"There was one thing — we all agree," the crow looked at the others as if to be sure of approval in his divulgence of information and, receiving no reprimand, continued. "Always we were thirsty."

"So thirsty!" another cried.

"Exceedingly thirsty!" said another as if yet mourning the very remembrance.

"So this is what you must do: Fill that jar there with water — See, there is a pump right there — and break it against the wall over your friend's head. He may hear the water rushing and rouse himself to drink."

Lala Lalu was not bred to argue, so he didn't. Promptly, he filled the jar with fresh water and broke the entire thing over his friend's head —

Ayaz's eyes snapped open. He had not even seen his friend standing beside him before he uttered the words "I am thirsty", and thus the vixen's spell was broken and Lala Lalu wasted no time in detailing her wicked ways. Nonetheless, she was now an angry vixen — glaring at them both and wide awake — with two giant guards at the door.

The vixen had been turning men into crows for her own amusement for a long time, and it was on account of her own cunning that she forgot how she had produced now her greatest threat. The crows greatly outnumbered her although the thought had never occurred to her; nonetheless, the crows had considered it several times and grew bolder with every occasion. It was she that put the murderous look in their eyes.

Thus Ayaz and Lala Lalu escaped as the crows swept down upon the vixen unrelenting in their attack

— pecking at her eyes, tearing at her lips, and ramming their beaks against her flesh. The two giant men, entirely preoccupied with quelling the attack upon her after she had screamed for their aid, did not even notice the young men's swift escape. And just as before, with the trapper's daughters, they did not stop running until they had reclaimed their horses in the woods.

"One thing is clear now, Lala Lalu," Ayaz said, panting, after they mounted their horses.

"Do tell." Lala Lalu coughed.

"She is *not* The Silent Princess."

Lala Lalu bristled, thinking about the bookcase. "How can you be sure?"

"My spirit is sure; I do not love that woman."

Chapter Five

As often as expectation beset Calah's heart, was it any wonder that she grew wholly disinterested in every suitor?

Consider Pasha Rosh. A beautiful man, as dark as the Black Sea, with skin that smelled as clean as cardamom and eyes that warmed the soul like cassia cinnamon, who first entered her receiving room dancing proudly in golden heels and swishing a tremendous cape and looking exceedingly interesting and astonishing. Even The Silent Princess could not deny that he'd stolen her high hopes at first sight.

"So, it's you," he said when he met her.

Calah stood at the center of the room dressed in textured reds and hammered silvers. His heels clicked against the tiled floor as he circled around her with the gait of an unhurried and proud pheasant and his decorated cape trailing behind — a buzzard-in-waiting. Still, his over-assured presence made the air feel as safe as standing next to a demigod, and she readily took to him without reason; and having noticed the smile in her eyes, Rosh hastened to take every advantage of her favor.

Immediately, he had papers drawn up that named her the sole Guardian of the Stars; then, he bequeathed his entire estate to her with ink and sealed documents;

and every day he danced for her, for he was the musical sort and very good at it too. By the end of the third day, he swore that his heart and soul belonged only to her — even if she never spoke.

'If only she would...'

Of course, there had to be an 'if only', for how could one pledge heart and soul to someone who could never pledge theirs back — or at least give answer to the proposal?

To his credit, Rosh waited another five days hinged upon 'if only'. He took her for walks in the garden, took her often in his arms to dance (though it was forbidden), played chess with her, and enjoyed many afternoon teas in her company. Nonetheless, a pasha can only leave his obligations unattended to woo a silent princess for so long, and eight days had seemed long enough to Pasha Rosh.

Tragically, just as Calah thought she might be willing to speak for him, however, Rosh sealed his own fate, finally betraying himself. Standing to leave her presence at the end of the eighth day, he turned upon her as a dog against its latest master and said:

"From the moment I arrived, I reasoned one sure way to get you to speak — and speak you will!"

And with these words he snatched an expensive and ornate silver necklace from Calah's neck with an evil grin and gloated as he stood over her, but the event he had been so sure would elicit a verbal response from the princess, had precisely the opposite effect and left The Silent Princess still silent.

She sat as straight as a pin and looked up at him, hurt; but as his grin turned into a frown, just as quickly, she despised his futile actions. No suitor since had disappointed her more; no suitor prior had lifted so high her hopes.

Always in a hurry to get there, always in a hurry to leave — none of the suitors ever believed that their fate would be the same as the rest. Such is the nature of human pride that boasts 'I am different'. And, she thought, he might have been — *different* — if not for such disloyal haste; but he had proven himself very much the same as the rest.

Rosh would not have been so proud of his golden heels had he known that they would be the cause of his untimely death between the colonnades. He slipped upon the smallest of puddles, placed by recent rains, the moment his heels met with the marble porch floor, and he fell down dead — another buzzard smacked with the reality of suddenly being prey within the realm that equalizes all men for a moment.

Still, Calah was a young woman and not a child now; she understood the value of breath and bone. So, she mourned for Rosh no less than the rest, even though he had caused her more hurt than he could have known.

The sultan was pleased. He had won an estate in the East without any cost to himself. He had Rosh's pretty corpse dumped, half naked, with the rest on the hillside that met the palace walls, where it landed about halfway down and was picked apart by crows and buzzards and dogs. His bones were eagerly polished clean by the sun...

Like the rest.

So it was that Calah learned that sight could be as pesky as speech, for all of the things a person couldn't see were as tiresome as all of the things a person did not say aloud — And wasn't Prince Efah another poignant example? Broad-faced with eyes as bright as blue moonbeams and milky skin, he entered in silence and soft leather shoes, and he sat in silence with her, and, truly, she had taken comfort in that for a time...

Yes, Efah's willingness to quiet himself alongside her had, at first, warmed her heart and tickled her skin. No milk-skinned people lived near The Silent Princess, so she thought he must have travelled a very long way only to sit in silence, and the fact that he had thought up such a clever approach was wholly endearing. Well, within the palace-world of sycophants, flatterers, liars, rulers, commanders, and whisperers, anyone might have found the prince's devices refreshing.

On the first evening, he poured her a glass of water and watched the sun set upon the west beside her on the balcony, then he left quietly. The second day, he sat next to her and read a book to himself silently. Sometimes he stopped and looked at her and smiled or offered her another drink. By the third day, they sat side-by-side contently sipping tea and watching the songbirds flit here-and-there; that evening, they sat and watched the stars dot-and-dash across the night sky — the sky affirming the season with a thousand twinkles in its eye.

The fourth morning sparkled with pale blue skies and promise, but Efah brought another book and sat contently reading it all morning. Calah, unable to sit another minute, got up and tried to pace the floor slowly so that her suitor might not notice her irritation, because she had something of a fancy for him but could not decide whether that was enough. He had not irritated her; he had not fawned over her; he had not smothered her with empty words; and all of these things were to his credit. Nonetheless, he just sat there and had sat there for days, and it was just this that she could not bear.

She beckoned the guards — who were always stationed just inside or outside of her chamber doors (today, inside) — with a simple nod of her head and just like that Prince Efah was shown out —

"What did I do?!" He yelled in a terrible soprano as they pulled him away.

Calah thought it was sad that he might never know that his fault was exactly that of doing nothing, but she was not willing to speak and entangle herself with him forever on account of his miscalculation, and so it was that Prince Efah died, same as the rest — though not before accusing her of misconduct, cursing her father, and spitting upon the palace guards.

What no one in the sultan's kingdom knew until the end, however, was that Prince Efah was prince of the

53

distant alien kingdom of shapeshifters. As he exited the castle, he transformed into a lion by which he thought to escape the mysterious fate of the other suitors, but in this too the prince was terribly mistaken. While he had been inside with the princess a wild bear had ascended to the yellow marble porch and, having already been discouraged — poked and cut — by the sultan's guards, the bear was in a blind rage when Prince Efah appeared on the porch, and the bear tore the lion apart into chunks.

Shapeshifters, having no form, die in the form in which they are killed, and that is how the rumor began that The Silent Princess had slain a lion who had called upon her — which, of course, was only partly true. Nonetheless, her infamy grew.

Now anyone understanding all that The Silent Princess had endured thus far might appreciate why she later donned a very long and elaborate veil over her head to cover the whole of her face. The veil upon her head was so ornate that she could scarcely see through it, and she wore it whenever another suitor appeared. She no longer wished to see what could be seen because what was unseen always seemed to weigh the greater portion of a soul. Though she could yet hear what was being said by the suitors, she seldom listened to their speeches because what was unsaid also seemed to weigh the greater portion of the character as well.

How different a princess she was now! All of the sultan's staff, and good Lili, looked upon her with great sorrow. Indeed, they now believed that the best thing would be for the poor girl to speak again. Anything, they imagined, might be better than her silence now! — For, week after week, they threw out the corpses of suitor after suitor, and the sight had become a permanent depression upon their thoughts, even if the sultan did not take it to heart.

Chapter Six

Sixteen long and meandering days after Ayaz and Lala Lalu had escaped the vixen, the mission — which had hardly begun — seemed to deserve a swift end. Ayaz had swallowed too many morose thoughts to encourage his friend, and his friend had swallowed too much badly-cooked fish and sour berries to want to be encouraged. In short, both men were ready to turn back and forget the whole thing, when they saw another woman. She was sitting gaily beside a stream splashing her feet and singing, thinking she was alone.

"Good day, woman," Lala Lalu said, greeting the woman after she had stopped singing.

She smiled with only a hint of surprise betrayed by her eyes and remained sitting beside the stream. "Good day."

Ayaz looked at Lala Lalu and shook his head in a warning. "We should keep moving this time."

Lala Lalu smiled his agreement but his mouth kept moving. "Woman, we are weary travelers on a strange mission. I wonder, have you heard of The Silent Princess? And, if so, could you point us in the right direction?"

" I heard she slew a lion, and all of her suitors end up dead too. Why would you want to go there?"

Ayaz shook his head *no* and Lala Lalu kept his mouth closed this time.

"Oh my," the girl replied. "You are suitors too?"

Now both men were exceedingly tired and the girl's words were heavier than they could bear on this particular day, for they had known nothing of The Silent Princess and her fame until now, and this new knowledge made their hearts faint. But Ayaz would not tolerate being badgered for the heartache he suffered, so he nudged his horse on, but Lala Lalu did not budge.

"Lala... Don't force my hand," Ayaz reprimanded, angered by his friend's stubbornness.

"Oh, please don't go." The girl stood. "May I ask you a question?"

Ayaz saw that he was outnumbered and, with a great sigh of annoyance, set down the reins on the horse's neck to let him graze.

"Oh, why not, Ayaz? We don't know where we're going anyway. I promise not to leave my horse," he added, smiling.

The girl looked pleased and so the young men waited to hear her.

"Why do you go to certain death when there are any number of maids you could have for wives in this forest?"

Had Ayaz known that women were so plentiful in the woods, he might have tried it sooner, but it would not do now.

"We've met a few of those maids; we'll take our chances, woman," Lala Lalu replied. "Do you know the way or not?"

"I know the way," she replied, "but I hate to send you on it. I've sent a few others before; they never return."

"That is their business," Ayaz replied, having no energy left to be offended nor frightened by the maid's words.

She shrugged and pointed south. "You have to travel three months that way, then you will come to the white Diamond Mountains. They will point the way from there."

"Three months?" Ayaz whined. "How did you come by this knowledge?"

"I was born in the white mountains. There is a village there, and everyone there knows about The Silent Princess."

Lala Lalu pointed his horse south. "Don't sour now that we have finally learned the way," he said, teasing Ayaz. "We are both to blame in not having it sooner."

Ayaz smirked. Lala Lalu was a good friend, and no matter how much Ayaz hated his words at times, he knew Lala Lalu was right. He took a deep breath, clutched the reins again, and addressed the girl.

"Thank you, woman. May we return the favor when our mission is done?"

The girl laughed. "I do not think you will be returning anything — but, if you do," she addressed Lala Lalu now, "come back for me."

Lala Lalu looked pleased and blushed and nodded.

"We should definitely keep moving now, Lala," said Ayaz, lurching his horse forward and laughing at his friend's reddened face.

"Good luck!" The girl called out, waving to them as they left.

"Won't need that!" Lala Lalu replied, waving back. "He's in love!"

Indeed, the young men's spirits were restored by having some direction now to point their horses and their hearts so that the rest of the day was spent laughing and teasing one another about certain death and certain love and treating their horses far kindlier than they had the sixteen days prior. But the maid in the woods spent the remainder of the day sulking; she knew the likelihood of their return — love or no love — and the husband who had brought her to this wood to live had died, so she was tired of sending away perfectly lovely suitors to a silent, stubborn, and slaying princess.

"You didn't get her name?" Ayaz asked his friend later that day.

"Not even a name," Lala Lalu answered.

"What kind of nincompoop promises to return for a maid he can't name?"

"The same sort of simpleton who thinks he can reason with a silent princess."

"Smitten and we don't even know their proper names," Ayaz mused, smiling again.

*

Soon after heading south, they left the woodlands behind, and spent the next month's crossing over the cooling grass plains and skirting the corners of a scrubby wasteland. Approximately three months later, they saw the glistening side of the Diamond Mountains come into view, as the woodland maiden had said, and they rejoiced to see a little village nestled upon its spine. The Diamond Mountains were the whitest and brightest they had ever seen, but they were not white with snow, though it was now the cold season. Some other mystery lightened the hills.

"Why do your hills glow white?" Ayaz asked a villager when they had reached the main road at the top.

"'Tis the brightness of The Silent Princess's soul, sir. Her soul is diamonds and diamonds are the first gift every suitor brings."

The villager, a tall man with earnest eyes, had answered matter-of-factly and pushed a cart loaded with coal past them. He never stopped. It was doubtful he could even identify the two strange men for he had scarcely looked at them as he passed. Ayaz and Lala Lalu were not accustomed to such indifference.

"Sir!" Ayaz called out after the man.

He waved a hand but never looked back —

"Plenty of diamond sellers in the city! Best of luck!"

Ayaz looked at Lala Lalu, who was shivering. "I don't want to buy diamonds," he said to Lala Lalu.

"We need to buy proper coats."

Ayaz shrugged. "Such a strange manner," he said, nodding in agreement with his friend as he turned his horse around and pointed him back to the village ahead. "I hope everyone in the town is not like that."

Had everyone in the Diamond Village been like that man, however, the two foreigners would not have noticed, because for every ten indifferent men hiding in the shadows, five eager-eyed, jolly, and compelling men stood to entice them to buy or sell or stay as they travelled through the heart of the village.

Whether the buyers and sellers were men native to the village, who could say? Many desirous of a profit had learned various means of prosperity along the routes leading to The Silent Princess, and many foreigners called these routes 'home 'periodically, seasonally, or residentially. Only those native to the Diamond Village could say who-was-who, of course.

When Lala Lalu spotted a sign boasting of fine furs, the young men dismounted and led their horses to his shop. Many market tables still lined the roadway, although many had moved their sales indoors due to the changing weather as the wind was biting that day.

"G'tidings, my friends! — Weary travelers in need of strong furs? — *Yes?* — Come, come!"

The owner of the shop, a stout mature man, waved them to the back corner where four chairs and a table made a sitting area. Grand fur coats — long, short, wide, trim, black, brown, grey, white, light, and dark — lined the walls conspicuously strewn across three large tables at the front and middle of the rectangular room.

"Sit! — I have just the thing!"

The owner pointed to the chairs and disappeared behind a curtain into a back room. Ayaz and Lala Lalu smiled, shrugged, and took seats, grateful to be in from the cold and welcomed so heartily by the strange and heftily mustached man. Having little need for money in the woodlands, they had plenty left for their journey and were eager to buy one of the warm wonders decorating the place. They sat comfortably, having thawed, wondering which coats might be theirs, when the owner returned sometime later with a tray in his hands and a large smile on his face.

"Coffee! — Just what two, cold, young adventurers need!"

Deciding that the man was not wrong, Ayaz and Lala Lalu took the tiny mugs and drank the strong, sweet drink down to the dregs. It was soon followed with Turkish Delight, and the men took this as a good sign; the shop owner had all of the good manners customary in their own city, and so they felt right at home.

Osmanek, the owner, soon began to entertain them with stories about all of the travelers and suitors that regularly passed by the Diamond Mountain village and told them many unbelievable tales, detailing how he had acquired the fascinating furs for his coats. Always there seemed to be the jaws of death snapping about him when he found a convenient dagger or a handy shard or, as in one tale, Osmanek managed to rip the throat of the creature out with his own teeth — but he swore they were all true stories. Even so, proving himself an entertaining storyteller, Osmanek convinced the two men to stay the night in his back room and leave with their new coats the next morn—

"The mountain passes are full of frights and it is dark now. Besides, you have another three month journey to reach the Ruby Mountains — that is where you must go next."

It was the 'another three month journey 'part that convinced them to rest there that night. Also, there were no fawning daughters present, so their situation seemed improved from the last time they had stayed the night with anyone, and, true to their suspicions, they slept wonderfully until morning light, enjoyed more coffee with their new friend, and purchased the most gorgeous winter coats that could be desired, for a fair price.

Now, it was true that Osmanek had seen his share of suitors passing through, but he liked Ayaz and Lala Lalu far more than the rest and so he gave them some fitting advice before they left.

"I make an honest living; I sell you what you need — Yes? — *Yes*. But others, they've learned how to cheat. So when they try to sell you diamonds for the princess, do not sell your warm coats for their diamonds!"

"Our coats for diamonds?"

"Yes, yes. *Don't you listen.* Just keep going. Liars and cheats; their lies will leave you frozen," he said wiggling a finger at them. "And anyway, the princess does not need diamonds! — *She needs a man!* — Yes?"

Osmanek laughed like an over-delighted child and slapped Ayaz's back.

"And coffee," Lala Lalu joked.

Osmanek's face stretched out to lengthen his laughter. "Yes! — And coffee!"

"Thank you for your hospitality," Ayaz concluded.

"You come back some time — bring the princess too!"

The younger men grinned and rode away wearing their new coats, unexpectedly thankful to have found a more optimistic informant. At least, Osmanek expected them back.

The morning was softer than the day before; the wind was less harsh. True to their new friend's counsel, five men and one woman tried to sell them diamonds for the princess before they were through the town — *and that was hardly a pleasure stroll's distance!* But the men took Osmanek's good advice and neglected to buy.

The men frowned and the woman scowled when the young men declined, and that was all Ayaz needed to know that he had made the right decision in not purchasing the diamonds. After hearing the stories about the suitors — what little Osmanek knew anyhow — Ayaz did not think diamonds would win The Silent Princess. She had probably been given those aplenty, he thought — so he began to think a lot about what would win such a princess over the next three month journey.

Chapter Seven

All of the men were fathers — the brothers having moved away due to the jealous attention of their wives — but Ayaz and Lala Lalu could not have known that when they approached the Ruby Mountain village. Had it not been for the bitter cold and recent snowfall, they would have been met by two dozen eligible young ladies seeking living suitors, as the Ruby Mountain village was too near The Silent Princess's own domain, and so there was a shortage of young men. Those who had not married local persuasions had gone off to court The Silent Princess (her father, long ago, giving up on being too choosy) and ne'er returned, and the consternation of the neglected women was visible in their half-fawning and half-despising eyes when any new suitor or stranger passed by.

However, darkness had locked all of the doors, and a thick snow had shushed all of the lights, when Ayaz and Lala Lalu arrived in town. A lone swinging sign that read The Ruby Mill above a lit room was the only quiet invitation they received, and they were overjoyed to have it after another harsh three months of travel.

Inside, a room full of salt-and-pepper beards sobered to look at the two young men enter. They did not get so many visitors in the winter months. One man, whose turn it was to greet strangers, cleared his throat and got up.

"Let's get these fine men a drink," he said, passing by the bartender and soon shaking the newcomers' hands.

"You must be exhausted. Have a seat," he said, pulling out a chair at an empty table.

"Thank you," Ayaz replied.

He pulled a chair up with them as the other men glared and returned to their drinking. "There're a few spare rooms above you can rent. How long are you here?"

"Just passing through," Lala Lalu answered.

"Uh-huh. Silent Princess then?"

"It seems we're getting closer," Ayaz said, trying to be nonchalant, annoyed but too tired to show it.

The bartender brought two drinks to the table, set them down, and pulled out what appeared to be a golden pepper mill. "Rubies?" he asked, holding the mill over their drinks.

Ayaz and Lala Lalu looked at each other and then at their seated host.

"Customary here," their host nodded. "Give them some."

The bartender pushed the handle around and a sparkling red powder fell into their drinks from the tiny mill.

"Is that really ruby?" Lala Lalu asked, mesmerized by the sparkles now floating in his glass.

"Gen-U-ine — and you can only get it here," the old-timer said, crossing his arms.

"Does it taste like anything?" Ayaz asked holding the glass mug up to inspect it.

"Does it taste like anything?" The man laughed and looked around the room; the others joined him in laughing.

"Like ruby red cheeks!" one shouted.

"The reddest lips you ever kissed!" another called out.

"Like coursing hot blood!" said another.

Their host scooted his chair closer and leaned in. "It's the stuff dreams are made of boys. Drink up!"

Ayaz nor Lala Lalu could acknowledge nor deny that the whole of Ruby Mill left them sitting uneasy in their chairs, so they drank despite their feelings against trying such strangely advertised things; but even they would tell each other later that they only drank the drink because they wanted to feel warm, as they were still chilled to the bone. Unheeded and uneasy suspicions, however, left them feeling tingly, then prickly, then sound asleep — and at the mercy of a whole town full of desperate fathers.

When the young men opened their eyes, brightened by rest and washed in warmth, the full splendor of the Ruby Village's wealth surrounded them with dazzling, ruby-studded, cerulean blue, tiled walls, set off by a waterfall of ruby-red velvet curtains that hung from ceiling to floor in their room. The curtains were open, splashing splendid amounts of late morning light on everything.

Ayaz and Lala Lalu looked at each other with hazy but happy wide-mouthed grins, though neither said a word. They sat in the enormous bed gazing at the wonders all around.

A red glass chandelier hung high over the room with hundreds of dangling little bluebird charms in flight. A giant, thick quilt of stitched leopard furs had kept them wrapped inside summer's arms despite winter's cold shoulder outside. Wooden planks as bright as the setting sun glowed orange and made up the floor, and the two men wondered how they had missed such lavishness upon entering the Ruby Mountain village; but they thought this room was above The Ruby Mill and did not yet realize that they had been moved to another location during the night in their slumber.

"These are the highest ceilings I've ever seen," Ayaz admitted.

"Exceedingly spacious," Lala Lalu agreed, nodding.

Pleased by the awakening splendors, the two men hurried to dress and find their benefactors, not yet recalling anything after first entering the tavern the night before on account of their weariness — or so they thought.

Only the locals knew that the milled rubies caused a temporary amnesia after consumption. It was very good to be a local... unless you were a woman in need of a husband, of course.

If planks like a cedar sun, blue tiles in the scent of a freshly mopped sky, and velvet red curtains are not appealing, then little more can be done to describe the majesty of the two-story chalet in which Ayaz and Lala Lalu found themselves. For a small village, the chalet might as well have been a palace and, though not nearly the size of a palace, it was not lacking in luxurious fixtures and highly polished details.

The stairs they descended from the bedroom opened up into a spacious kitchen and lounging area. The pleasing odor of coffee and orange had already filled the rooms.

"Where are we?" Lala Lalu asked, bewildered.

Ayaz shook his head, dumbfounded by the unexpected and unknown quarters. "Heaven?"

Just then the front door opened, but it wasn't God or Saint Peter who appeared. No, it was the same old-timer who had greeted them the previous night and he entered with a sly grin.

"Well rested, wayfarers?"

"Wonderfully so!" Lala Lalu burst. "But what is this place?"

"Well," the man paused to scratch his beard, "we built it for a prince who promised to stay and govern the village, but he left us in the lurch just before we finished."

"Sounds like a soursop," Ayaz replied, warming his hands at the open hearth fire.

"Well…" The local's eyebrows shot up but good humor extended one corner of his mouth. "Some womenfolk are bringing food. Stay as long as you like." He threw his hands up, "No one lives here anyway. Sits empty most of the year."

Ayaz and Lala Lalu marveled at their good fortune and reflected on their past adventures after the man left. A long, solid, highly-polished wooden table sat in front of the hearth. Ten sturdy, lion-pawed chairs of wood, lined with more leopard fur, sat around the table. A smaller hearth for cooking was at the back of the room. A flashy brass cauldron hung in the hearth and a smaller table, with all sorts of utensils, bowls, and domed plates, stood beside it. The giant beams of exposed rafters interlocked like fingers overhead.

"What sort of prince leaves such a place?" asked Ayaz, still gawking.

Lala Lalu poured the ready-made coffee from a small pitcher into two small bronze cups and smiled at his witless friend, who had already seated himself in the lounging area on a gorgeous sapphire blue couch. *He could imagine just the sort of prince —*

"One who came from a bigger castle."

"One man's castle, another man's parlor — I see." Ayaz chuckled.

"My mother always said comparison was a useless venture of always gathering and never having," Lala Lalu answered, carrying the cups to the sitting area's round table and sitting down next to his friend.

"Your mother was wise."

Halfway through their coffee, a light tap rang from the large rectangular front doors. Lala Lalu opened it, bowed slightly, and opened wider. A young woman, dripping with enough jewels to make the Queen of Sheba jealous and carrying a large domed platter of food, stepped in with a lightness of foot that would have made even Midas 'touch turn green. She inspired the men, being the first of the Ruby Village's women that they had seen. Going straight to their round lounge table, she set the domed platter down in front of Ayaz and lifted the lid, beaming.

"Sausages, potatoes, and toast. I hope you like it," she added, blushing.

Ayaz stared up at the little bedecked princess, speechless. White-blonde hair piled up, layer after layer, and wrapped with gold and silver wire, sat upon her head like a crown and provided a resplendent contrast to her doe-colored skin.

"It's the best thing we've seen in months," Lala Lalu assured the woman, nodding sincere appreciation. He spoke of the food — *there was a hierarchy about such things after all, and they were very hungry* — but he wondered if Ayaz had even seen the plate yet, so rapt was he with the vision of feminine decadence.

"I'll get the plates," she said, blushing.

She was already moving towards the small kitchen as the words dangled behind her. Bringing two plates and three forks, she filled each man's plate.

"Please eat," she said when she was done.

"Please join us," Ayaz spilled. "Tell us of your village life here."

Her sweet chin tilted with a nod and a smile broke the room like sunrise every time she donned it. She decorated a darling loveseat across the table from the two strangers. A lightweight sheer parka shrugged with her shoulders, as she began.

"I am Emra Esmerelda. I have two sisters, and I have lived here my whole life. I think you met my father. What would you like to know?"

Now Ayaz and Lala Lalu had grown weary with many trials along the way, and their resolve grew thin; indeed, what else could have explained the rush of betraying thoughts — slicing mission from intention — compromising their stated loyalties at the very sight of this Emra? For she was lovely, endearing, and dressed in such finery, and the chalet was so regal and captivating, that the young men could hardly think of a single reason to leave the Ruby Mountain or the sight of such precious things.

It is well and good to resist temptation when things are less than what is desired, but it is a feat of extraordinary grace and faith to deny temptations when they appear as perfections. The Ruby Village's Prince Chalet and the Ruby Mountain's Emra embodied perfection in both men's momentary estimation, and a glittery fog settled between their ears such as they had never before known.

The sausages were especially good.

"Why didn't the prince stay? — You are so beautiful."

The words left Ayaz's mouth in a moment of succinct satisfaction with the sausages and he could not stuff them back inside, though his cheeks brightened slightly. "I apologize for being too transparent," he quickly added.

Emra's songbird-blue eyes plunged into a delicately rimmed bath, as her eyelids fluttered. "Please don't apologize. No one says such nice things here."

"They must be blind," Lala Lalu growled.

Emra looked uncomfortable and shifted in her seat. Her eyelashes flashed like sparkly hummingbird wings, and just as fast, but soon came to rest as the bath air-dried and she regained composure.

"I was offered to the prince. He accepted. This house was built for us."

Ayaz coughed on a piece of toast.

"The fiend…" Lala Lalu inserted his opinion about the prince while patting his choking friend's back.

The bedazzled princess looked down into her lap.

"I've lost my appetite. The very thought spoils it," Ayaz stated, setting his plate aside.

"Is it so very terrible here, princess? — Please tell us."

Lala Lalu addressed her in earnest wondering what would possess such a man to leave all they had seen — despite his prior comments about princes and castles — holding just slightly more honest suspicion than his friend.

Her eyes darted up.

"Oh no! You must not think that! This is a *wonderful* place!" She defended. "The summer warmth well makes up for the bitterness of winter, with all kinds of birds and beasts filling it with song; and the river below is clear and strong; and the jewels are like stones here — they are so plentiful! The Ruby Mountain is a wonderful place, though the wayfarers hardly know it. They never stop long enough to know it," she concluded, looking down again. "Like the prince; they just never stop long enough."

"But he agreed?" Ayaz persisted.

"Yes," she sighed. "He stayed here for three months. I suppose he should have known it, but he was a prince. He had seen far more of the world than I; Ruby Mountain is all I know. To him, this was too much and not enough all at once."

"Too much and not enough?"

She flashed a terse grin at Lala Lalu before answering.

"He had castles; we have a chalet. He could have hundreds of wives and concubines; we only have two dozen."

Her narrow shoulders shrugged again, as if shirking the retelling of a common myth — as if everyone knew because she knew.

"Only? Dozens?" Ayaz asked, clearing his throat and sitting up neater.

"Yes. That was part of the deal. I am the wife, the princess — if you prefer. My sisters and the other daughters of the town are the concubines: Our fathers insist that we all go together since men are so scarce."

The men's faces blanched. Emra wrung her hands in her lap, seeing their surprise; she thought her father had already told them.

"Oh, you must understand," she blurted, pleading now. "Every suitor passes through but none stay, and all the men have left us here to wither in old age! *Whom shall I marry? Whom shall my sisters marry?* There is no one here but our mothers and fathers. Oh, please see that we need you — you could both be our husbands and split the burden."

Well, the grief-stricken princess was nearly in tears and the men found her even more endearing in the act. *How could they begrudge her desire? How could they despise her pain?* Yes, they understood, and they understood that they had fallen far too in love with the whole idea the instant they had woken up in the chalet and seen the dear girl; that is to say that they understood that their feet had left the ground and suspended their heads in the clouds. Neither knew what course to take.

Finally, Ayaz spoke to console the girl who still looked distraught from her outburst, though no less lovely.

"These are heavy matters," he replied softly. "Give us time to think these things through?"

She nodded, but it was a nod of defeat. She ran from the chalet.

"That old-timer is a sly fox. This is worse than the trapper's daughters," Lala Lalu stated, wide-eyed.

"This is worse than the vixen's crows," Ayaz admitted. "I see now that those were trials but not hardly the temptation that this is!"

"For once, we agree."

There were choices to be made. The mystery of The Silent Princess haunted Ayaz and he desired to solve it, but that mystery had lost its urgency along the way. Emra's case, however, was urgent — *wasn't it?*

Chapter Eight

Growing increasingly melancholy, Calah began refusing all food except bread and drinking only grape juice. Good Lili begged her to take more and every suitor offered her delicacies from their own lands or families, but she refused. No longer did she observe the afternoon tea, and this upset the staff the most; it was tradition, after all. Every day, she sat out on the balcony wrapped in thick blankets and mulled over her life, the heaviness of it all. Every evening, Lili pulled her inside and put her to bed. In many ways, she became in manner like a small child again.

The princess assessed that she could not speak rightly, so how could she ever speak again? She could not bear the weight of the veils; thus, she could not bear the weight of yet another misspoken word. A single outburst had led to a curse, seven veils, hundreds of dead suitors, and years of rejection, fear, fakery, or scorn from others. That was a heavy price to pay for one childish misdeed — wasn't it? *Weren't the untold consequences of one sin enough to fill a lifetime with remorse?* Why would anyone keep to their course under the weight of such knowledge? Like King David's numbering of the Israelites, weren't thousands of dead men enough?

King David had continued living, but Calah wasn't sure she could. She had caused enough damage, and she could not bear the memory of her mother's disappointment and her father's disregard much longer. She despised herself well enough — *knowing that with every judgment of a suitor, she had been guilty of double judgment against herself* — without the repeated personal blows of their bruised and broken remembrances.

She could not wish her grandmama well now.

She could not say goodbye to her mother.

She could not resurrect the dead.

She could not make the sultan see her pain.

She could not bear to speak.

And she could not see how her life wasn't already over.

But who would have guessed such thoughts for someone so pretty and so stubborn? Calah sat curled up against lavish cushions, draped in finely embellished blankets, her neck, wrists, and ankles, adorned in jewels, watching the sun set behind the distant trees from a yellow marble palace. She was hardly the picture of despair despite her strange circumstances. When a sweet breeze blew a smile onto her face, her thoughts disappeared entirely behind the extravagant facade to the passing observer.

But Calah thought to kill herself.

Chapter Nine

The choice was now, not later — if, indeed, he had one.

If he stayed in the Ruby Mountains, if he married the bedecked and darling Emra, would he fall ill again wondering later about The Silent Princess? That prospect was wholly unfair to the women of the Ruby Village.

Yet, if he left and failed in his quest with The Silent Princess — *a highly probable outcome* — was his death worth the loyal quest? Surely a triumph would be worth the reward, but, even then, he only supposed with naked hope, not certainty.

Which would he regret most? Or was it that he would regret *this* because he had *that* and regret *that* because he kept *this*?

After several hours of agony teetering on like this in his own mind, Ayaz decided regret was a terribly fickle thing entirely insubstantial in matters of choice. He reasoned that he shouldn't give the proposal any less examination than if he were buying a horse; he wanted to know something of the pedigree: he wanted to talk to the fathers and mothers of the Ruby Village.

It was to their credit, after all, how they had proposed the situation. Ayaz could well imagine the far less pretty and far more binding scenarios that could have ensnared him after the ruby drink. They seemed a fair and reasonable people who deserved at least a hearing — even if it wasn't what he had intended upon starting his journey. Some things were certain, and some things were not; but Emra was flesh and blood and that, he thought, had to count for something more than his fickle thoughts.

Lala Lalu found the old-timer at The Ruby Mill and asked him to summon the people and the eligible young women to the chalet for a meeting. The men, quite surprised by the invitation, enlivened, fetched their wives and their dear girls, who were all equally pleased. Soon, the dazzling chalet was several degrees warmer and fuller. There was so little room now that Ayaz and Lala Lalu stood on the shiny dining table to address them all and, from that view, the two dozen ladies-in-waiting were put under quiet spotlight. They could see that all of their faces were full of anticipation.

Little more could be said of the meeting, however, because before he could speak, Ayaz's body lost all muscle — like a dream that leaps from the heart and seizes upon the neck, a sudden flash of remembrance struck Ayaz's whole body as he stood looking out at the crowd and, as it shook him, the room blurred and he fell flat across the table as if dead.

"Ayaz!"

Lala Lalu leapt down from the table and joined more than one mother already lifting his head and hands and checking for a pulse, as he had fallen straight down upon his breast and belly.

"He is alive," one of the mothers assured Lala Lalu, nodding and patting the young man's back. "Let the men move him up to the bed. The pressure was too much, I think," she added. "It is too much for any man."

Lala Lalu nodded, bewildered and shocked.

Three fathers (one who was the village doctor) and Lala Lalu moved Ayaz back upstairs, where the doctor examined him more thoroughly and concluded that the sensation was no more than a fainting spell, a head swell: "His head is swollen with curses and concerns," he said.

"Curses?" Lala Lalu burst taking up a defensive position for his unconscious friend.

The older man's brown eyes twinkled and put Lala Lalu at ease, even against his own will. The doctor had been doctoring souls for a long time in the Ruby Mountains; he was familiar with such ills, though they befell men in differing ways.

"Well, curses or blessings; it can be hard to tell at first. Much depends upon the ground of the man. Thorns and thistles of mind and heart…"

The doctor looked down at Ayaz's body again, then continued. "This one wears a crown of thorns; it's digging in — Does he ever do any digging?"

Lala Lalu found the doctor's words a complete riddle and shrugged.

The doctor touched his hand to his lips and nodded, as if expertly interpreting the shrug. For all Lala Lalu knew, he was doing just that.

"Well," the doctor finally continued, throwing his hands in the air, "time will tell. Until then, let him rest a while."

The townsfolk left after the doctor — first the disappointed young women, followed by the worried mothers, herded by the rest of the disgruntled fathers, who thought the entire event to be a bad omen and now wondered how they might get the two young men to leave town.

A little digging dream later, Ayaz's eyelids flung themselves open wide as he regained consciousness. He sat straight up to address his friend who sat at the end of the bed.

"We cannot stay" were his first words.

Lala Lalu blinked twice, then nodded. "I suppose I knew as much, but it took your fainting to assure me of it."

"But how do we leave now? How do we leave these people in such disappointment?"

"Emra left a few minutes ago; let me tell you what she told me," Lala Lalu answered.

"Do, dear Lala! — And tell me it is good news!"

"She told me that the fathers no longer wish us to stay. They took your fall as a bad sign of weakness."

Lala Lalu accentuated his words with a grin at the end, but seeing that Ayaz was shocked by this, he continued. "Being wise, she asked only a promise that we would send good men back to them after we are well-situated with your silent princess."

Ayaz tilted his head and a smile slipped towards the lower half of it. "She is a dear and wise girl, isn't she? It is too bad that she isn't The Silent Princess herself! — But I will consider that no more."

Lala Lalu saw his friend's face turn serious again and waited to listen.

"I saw the old woman — I heard her words again — and I saw the princess's face before I fell. It struck me like lighting!"

"But you've never seen her."

"I know! But I did see her somehow…"

"Was she pretty?"

Ayaz shook his head, annoyed. "That is not the point, Lala; I saw her soul. I saw that she is like a treasure hidden in a field — you remember that story, of course?"

"I do, but I don't understand."

Ayaz peeled back the covers he'd been placed under and began putting his boots back on. "The circumstances are undesirable — the length of this journey, the various temptations, the many times we could have forsaken it — it's like a plain-clothed, hard and rocky, field. But the treasure beneath…" He lifted his smiling head, boots donned, and took a deep breath.

Lala Lalu thought his friend might be insane, but he permitted him this leeway because of the old widow's words and all of the strange prior rejections; yes, he supposed his friend was within his rights to be slightly mad, so he said nothing.

"I am sure I must go to her," Ayaz finished.

Lala Lalu nodded. "Then I am sure also. There's not much else we can do; they mean to throw us out if we don't leave."

"Then let's not waste heart!"

Emra saw that the favored two young men were provisioned and had whatever they required for the final leg of their journey to The Silent Princess.

"When you see the yellow marble castle and the white hill, you will know you've arrived."

"Thank you, dear Emra. And we will keep our promise to you," Ayaz replied.

She blew them a kiss as they left, unwavering in her belief that they would keep their word to her if at all possible... if they were not killed by the strange and silent princess. Even so, she believed.

"This is a good journey for us," Lala Lalu commented later, as his beautiful roan horse swayed him gently down another hill.

Ayaz listened quietly, his horse a few paces ahead, knowing that whatever comment Lala Lalu began aloud, he would eventually finish aloud. This was true even when the lapse lasted for days. Thankfully, this time, he only waited mere seconds.

"Think of the dear people we met along the way — people we could have been stopped by and entangled with had we not so certain a mission and fidelity of mind. The woodland maiden, Osmanek, the dear Ruby Village and its precious Emra: did we not love them all?"

"I believe it was you who loved the woodland maiden, and I think you've already forgotten how easily good food swayed us from fidelity," Ayaz grinned.

Lala Lalu took a deep breath. "You're insufferable."

Ayaz looked back at his friend and nodded.

"What I mean is, the choices are overwhelming. Without a purpose in mind, it must be terribly easy to do — *well* — anything! To be entangled with anyone we find engaging at the time; I think we've found that much to be true."

"I like the way you say that, Lalu."

His friend smiled and sat a little taller. He felt honored by Ayaz's admitted respect.

"When I become king, I'll be sure to write that down and pass it off as my own quote," Ayaz said, stopping to look his friend in the eye.

Lala Lalu scowled and poked his heels into his horse, trotting ahead.

"The doctor was right: your head is swollen!" he yelled back.

Ayaz, suddenly aware that he did not remember a doctor nor what was said while under his spell, urged his horse to catch up, yelling: "Hey! What did the doctor say? — I command you to tell me!"

Lala Lalu laughed and encouraged his horse into a frolicking gallop across the powdered and windswept valley.

Chapter Ten

It was April, springtime, when the yellow marble castle finally came into view. A fresh, heavy snow had fallen so that all of the hills were clothed in white. A hot-headed sun glinted off of the gold-domed castle in the distance, adding to the already blinding effect of the reflective snow. Ayaz and Lala Lalu were forced to look away from the yellow marble, set up to their right on a hill, and turned their attention back towards their path. It was a small road that curved around the bottom of the hill and disappeared into a forested-crest ahead, only visible now by the hooves and footprints of the few who had gone before them.

Lala Lalu stopped to rub the same spot in his back he'd been rubbing since about a week after they had begun their journey ten months ago.

"Women don't know how much we endure for them," he griped, shaking his head. "If I don't find a suitable bed for a week, I think this ligament is going to snap."

"Have you endured for a woman or for a friend?" Ayaz asked, as he rubbed his achy forearms.

Lala Lalu conceded with a nod and a smile.

"We look terrible," Ayaz said, examining what he could see of himself from the front.

"It's a wonder we have any stitch of clothing left; it's a good thing we have these coats!" Lala Lalu replied.

The nearness of their destination brightened both men's countenances as they spoke.

"Yes, but it's almost too warm for them now," Ayaz answered, pulling his horse forward. They had grown weary of riding.

As they reached the crest of the path, surrounded by trees, they could see the city situated below in a pretty valley. Large, round fires burned a clear path through the city's heart, where the colorful, striped coverings of an outdoor marketplace came into view. Another path connected, just ahead, that led up to the castle.

"So close, yet so far." Ayaz mused, as his eyes wandered back up, through the trees, where the gold dome was still visible.

Lala Lalu put a hand on his friend's shoulder. "We should learn what we can in the city first; they will know far more about the situation."

As they entered the city below, the first thing Ayaz saw in the covered village marketplace was all of the caged birds — beautiful birds, crested, breasted, ringed, and bedazzling birds — all glorified with soft greens, sharp reds, sophisticated yellows, with slices of brown, black, blue, and purple. Perhaps that's what made her stand out —

The nightingale might have been called drab next to the others, but there was something about the eyes, something about the way she held herself, and something about her song that was far lovelier than the other squawking and strutting birds. Before he could think another thought, and while Lala Lalu was looking at vests, Ayaz exchanged a small ruby from Emra for the nightingale and received some currency back as it was a very nice ruby.

Lala Lalu saw them both and crossed his arms to restrain his disdain. "We have enough of a burden without a bird."

"If you knew how much it blesses me, you would not say such," Ayaz replied, undeterred, because Lala Lalu did not know that his friend had desired such a bird since before he broke the old widow's pitchers; and such childhood longings are not easily put away.

The second thing they noticed was that there were plenty of young men out and about. This thing also encouraged them.

With the rest of their coin spent on finding a room and a little food, and leaving the nightingale in their room, the two men set out to gather what information they could regarding the princess. Despite the dead weight of the heavy snow, light hearts and bright eyes and snowflake-glittered children were making merry, resting in the hopes of the coming season. Though the snow was fresh, the wind was warming fast into Spring; at least half of the townspeople were out enjoying their labors, and that was ten times as many as all of the people in the Ruby Village. The Golden Valley, as they learned the city and location were called, was no small thing, for the kingdom had prospered greatly — for better or worse — under the spell of The Silent Princess.

After an hour of loitering about and listening, Ayaz and Lala Lalu realized one very important thing: *No one in the Golden Valley spoke of The Silent Princess.*

Ayaz stopped a man carrying firewood. "Excuse me. Could you tell me something of The Silent Princess?"

The man grunted and shook his head but gave no answer.

Next, they asked a woman who had a table of soaps for sale.

"Ungrateful child, if you ask me," she answered. "But it's good for business."

Shrugging, she ducked back inside a tent behind her table, then returned with two handsome daggers. She smiled widely and thrust the daggers towards the men. "If I were you, I'd buy these and stab her heart the moment you see her. You won't get a better fate anyway. Such a spoil seeing good men go to waste on account of one spoiled brat."

Ayaz and Lala Lalu backed away, shook their heads *no*, and returned to their rented room after receiving a half dozen more similar replies from various merchants.

"These people do not have much good to say about her," Lala Lalu commented when they were alone again. "Should that concern you?"

Ayaz picked up the nightingale and smiled. "Perhaps they don't know much," he answered, softly.

"Perhaps, they know *too* much," the nightingale answered.

"It talks!" Lala Lalu put down the poker he was using to stir a small pot of stew over a small fireplace in their room.

"Well, I don't crochet and one must have something to do," the bird replied.

Ayaz's eyes lit up. "One who speaks should not be caged," he said, opening the cage door.

The nightingale jumped from the perch and flew a short distance, landing on the back of a chair nearby. "Thank you, sir. I knew you were a soul of dignity the moment you looked at me."

"You are most welcome, nightingale; but what did you mean when you said that perhaps they know *too* much?" Ayaz asked.

The fireplace cast the bird in a tawny light and made her eyes glisten like obsidian. Lala Lalu and Ayaz now sat with rapt attention upon the edge of the bed — on the edge of a bed in a room in the inn, in the inn on a street in the city, in the city of the Golden Valley, in the Golden Valley beneath the watery, starry heavens God had made, listening intently to the dear nightingale.

"Imagine a girl who spends her whole life looking out of a window at a city below; imagine the things that she will observe over time; imagine the assumptions, the perspectives, and the bird's-eye-view her heart will piece together if she is only ever permitted to look. Not touch."

"I see," Ayaz replied, somberly.

"Do you?" the nightingale challenged. "Imagine now that this girl has everything on a golden platter; she has tea served in the finest of china; her every gown is a priceless wonder — no two alike. Baubles and fine instruments, silk dolls and pastry delights, she has the world over. Imagine also a girl who has heard all of the nicest of words and all of the worst too — and that she has only known all of these words from behind yellow marble walls. Yes, imagine that everything around her is priceless, while she remains held to ransom by that which she most desires."

"What does she most desire?" asked Lala Lalu.

"What else but to be seen, to be heard — to be treated with the same care and preciousness as those things around her?"

"To be forgiven of her sins as she learns to forgive," Lala Lalu nodded, stately, arriving at his own conclusions.

The nightingale nodded respectfully to him. "You are a keen friend," she replied.

But Ayaz's face was frozen; two streams of tears fell down it, trickling out bits of his heart. "I am just a suitor like any other, dear nightingale; how can I win this silent princess? How can I hear her if she will not speak? How can I see her if she insists upon being veiled?"

(Osmanek had told them about the veils she wore, though no one knew the real reasons she wore them.)

The nightingale lowered her head and seemed to smile. In this new position, her eyes were like glowing apples in settings of silver by the firelight.

"Brave suitor, take cheer; I see that you do not know too much. Take me with you to the castle and I will help you."

Chapter Eleven

Good timing has cheated death at least as often as poor timing has caused it. Thankfully, Ayaz's journey, however convoluted or strange, bore the marks of good timing. Ayaz could not bear to wait another day when the nightingale promised help, so they had gone up to the castle that very evening — and it was a good thing too.

Even so, it was a visit that might not have happened if not for Ayaz's courage. In talking to the nightingale, he had missed the first pathway up to the castle and, thus, had to climb up the west side of the hill. As he ascended, he realized that his feet were crunching and sinking a great deal more than they should in the snow, and, upon further examination, he discovered that he was walking upon skeleton bones.

His face blanched, as he said, "I think these are the suitors who have come before us."

Thankfully, he had the nightingale's encouragement," We could suffer the same fate."

"We won't know unless we go, will we?" Ayaz replied. And after this exchange, they went up the hill in silence.

After Ayaz received the sultan's approval to entertain The Silent Princess, good Lili knocked upon the princess's chamber door at the very moment Calah held the cold point of a dagger against her own skin and meant to plunge it — a gift from Efah — into her own chest. Instead, she sighed, put the dagger away, and tidied up her room to receive yet another suitor. It was late in the day, but there were still a few hours left of the social night.

Lili had announced that a man named 'Ayaz 'was on his way to see her, and — truth be told — Calah was glad of the excuse not to harm herself; after all, there was nothing wrong with her body, only the terrible inside ache and a deceptive veil. So, she reclined upon the plethora of pillows on her couch and waited. A young man with beautiful dark curls, wearing the most ridiculously oversized fur coat, entered quietly and stood for a moment staring at her — as far as she could tell through her veiled headdress.

Ayaz bowed and shuffled the nightingale to a large candlestick beside the balcony doors as he introduced himself:

"Dear princess, my heart overflows upon finally learning your name: Calah. I am Ayaz of Wargwherlandia and I've travelled many months to find you."

The young man continued on, telling of his travels and trials in coming to see the princess — as so many men had done before and as so many are prone to do because of some social training — but The Silent Princess hardly heard a word. Still, Ayaz did not permit himself to think too poorly of her behavior since he quite understood how difficult it was to listen when one had heard so much already.

He had heard two dozen rejections in the past, and he had always caught their drift by the end of the opening lines and tuned out early too in such times. So, after a few minutes of such required pleasantries, Ayaz decided it was time to put the nightingale to the test.

"Well, since I have travelled so far," he began, "and since you seem determined to permit my fate to be as the rest before me, I will talk now to the candlestick. Why should I come so far and not at least leave with a good conversation?"

At 'talk now to the candlestick', Calah's ears regained consciousness, and her eyebrows raised slightly at this new entertainment. For certain, no one had tried that before.

"Oh, dear candlestick, how are you this fine evening?"

The nightingale, hidden away on a small rim near the bottom of the candlestick replied: "I am well, good man. Thank you for speaking with me. It has been a long time since anyone spoke to me."

"You are quite welcome," Ayaz replied, amused. "I imagine that it has been even longer since anyone has listened to you."

"So right you are, good man! So, pray, sit and let me tell you a story that demands some consideration."

"You honor us, candlestick! What a wonderful idea. I will sit and listen."

Ayaz sat down at the other end of the couch. Calah sat up, for he had nearly sat on her feet, and pulled her legs under herself with a little gasp only the veil heard.

"There once lived a lovely princess who could not decide upon a suitor. And I want you to know that it was not because she was a naughty princess but only a slightly-too-bright one that she was undecided.

"See, this princess had very carefully studied her friends and her relatives, her acquaintances and the strangers who passed through the kingdom, and upon studying she began to realize the futility of choice. It seemed to this princess that one could choose a good mate who then turned out to be quite wicked in the end or one could make a lesser choice that then turned out to be a very fine match in later years. And so it was, that she found choosing a suitor an impossible choice of chance and luck, so she neglected the duty because she was afraid she would regret her choice no matter which one she made."

"I see. That is a dilemma," Ayaz replied.

"Yes," the nightingale answered. "Well, being strongly pestered by the king and queen to make a choice, the dear princess fell into a terrible nightmare from which she could not escape, and no one could wake her. Night after night, she moaned and writhed upon her bed, and sometimes screamed, but there seemed no remedy to her malady.

"Eventually, however, word reached three men in a neighboring kingdom of the princess's state, and they made a pact to wake her — each with his own special skill — and, thereby, one of them might win the fair princess's hand.

"Now, Egan knew that he could repel the princess's nightmares, and Soshi foresaw that the princess would soon die and, thus, provided the wisdom to their haste; and Gorson had the talent of supernatural transportation. So it was that Soshi was first to see the princess's dire need; Gorson was the one to transport the three men to her side with haste; and Egan was the one who, upon arrival, delivered the princess from her terrible nightmares, and she sat up wide awake after many months in such a state. But now, who should the princess choose to marry?"

Ayaz cocked his head and bounced his eyebrows. "Well, without Gorson to transport them to the princess, they could not have succeeded, so she should choose Gorson."

"Ah, but what about Soshi? If he had not foreseen her need for immediate deliverance, they would not have arrived in time. Shouldn't she then choose Soshi?"

Ayaz and the candlestick argued back and forth about this for some time, one saying Gorson should be chosen and the other insisting that Soshi was the one.

And they went on bickering until The Silent Princess could bear their short-sightedness no longer —

"That isn't right! Without Egan who delivered her from the nightmares, the first two are positively useless! She must choose Egan!" Calah burst.

The veil ripped. *Only a little.* But everyone in the room heard it.

Ayaz smiled.

Calah stood up, alarmed.

Good Lili, who was standing by the door and heard the whole affair, sent the soldiers to tell the sultan what happened, and he came immediately.

"What is this? Dear daughter? Is it true?"

Calah held up two of her fingers and insisted (through gestures) that Ayaz must make her speak twice more to win her, and though this was not to the sultan's liking, all agreed, for at least some progress had been made.

Ayaz bid her goodnight, slyly retrieving the dear nightingale and left.

Calah spent the rest of the night wondering why the veil had torn — dragging her emotions between terror and delight.

Chapter Twelve

The following night, hidden behind a pillar and after the same procedures as the night before, the nightingale began to convey this story to The Silent Princess and her suitor:

"There are some princesses who need a suitor chosen and a good spanking if you ask me," began the pillar. "But tell me what you think; I once heard the story of a princess called Cruel. She really put men to the test, yet the tests never concluded with her making a choice, only more tests. Even so, the princess, Cruel, had three persistent suitors who could see nothing of her flaws but saw only her beauty and, thus, subjected themselves to her tests repeatedly. But here is the last one conveyed to me,,

"The princess wished to test the three suitors again, promising a decision, so she told one of the suitors, Rhys, that her father's fate was in his hands. She lied and told him that if he didn't lie inside a freshly dug grave all night that her father would die and immediately fill the space in the ground. Being entirely at Cruel's will, Rhys immediately dug a grave outside of her palace window and laid down in it.

"Princess Cruel, amused, laughed to herself and called in the suitor called Thum. She told him that an evil spirit had come to her and told her of her father's death. 'He lays in the ground now', she told him. 'And if he awakens and stirs, then the evil spirit will come for me too!'

"Thum, quite alarmed by this, asked the princess what he must do, so she told him to take a hatchet and stand guard over the grave all night. 'If the corpse moves, you must stick the hatchet in its head or I will be lost', she told him. And, of course, he went dutifully to conduct his mission in behalf of her life, as it was now dark and he could not see that it was Rhys in the grave. Both men were too frightened of their missions to speak.

"Durk was then summoned to the princess, Cruel, who told him that Death himself was standing over her father's grave with a hatchet and that he must cut down the branch of the tree hanging over their heads lest Death snatch her father's corpse from the grave and spoil his remains.

"Durk, being more loyal than bright, and passionate for the princess's favor, immediately went out and secured an axe, climbed the tree, and began sawing at the large branch hanging overhead."

"What great faith these suitors had in their princess!" Ayaz exclaimed at last. "I can scarcely bear to hear another word of it!"

"Yes. Unbeknownst to the princess, however, her father, the king, had seen the entire affair and guessed as to his daughter's game; thus, he decided he would choose a suitor from the three men for her before they were killed by her childishness. But whom should he choose? I think Durk is most deserving because his pure loyalty needed the least excuse."

"Now, wait; don't you think poor Thum is worth some consideration? After all, holding a hatchet overhead all night is no small task," Ayaz volleyed with twinkling eyes.

The pillar, which was the nightingale, and Ayaz went on like this for some time arguing about whether the king should choose Durk or Thum for the princess, Cruel, and also arguing about whether she was deserving of any man.

Calah tried to restrain herself, but the inferiority of their arguments was too much to bear at last, and she blurted:

"Why can't you clearly see that Rhys was put at the most mortal danger and, thus, is the most deserving? — If she deserved any at all!"

"So, we agree that perhaps she deserved none of them?" Ayaz smiled.

The veil ripped again. It was tearing from the bottom up and about half of it was torn now.

Again, the sultan was summoned and, again, Ayaz bowed, slyly retrieving the nightingale as he had before and left promptly, lest his own princess change the rules of the game and he overstay his welcome.

*

At dusk the following night, Ayaz hid the nightingale in the folds of the lavish curtains in Princess Calah's room and took a seat next to her on the couch again. Once more, he began with the customary pleasantries, commenting upon how lovely she looked and how pleased he was to see her again and upon receiving no reply to these things, he proceeded to have a discussion with the curtains.

"Well, dear curtains, I don't know who else to talk to. Perhaps you have something to say?"

"What great courtesy you show to amuse me in conversation. I have hung here for years upon years and no one else has ever shown me such courtesy. So, I will reward you with my own story to tell. Yes, I have an unusual story too; one does not hang around so long without having stories to tell you know."

Ayaz laughed. "Please, go on, dear curtain. I will listen."

"Ah, my story is a tragedy, I'm afraid. Indeed, I still do not know what to think about it myself."

"Oh, please go on; I will help you sort it out if I can," Ayaz replied.

"Certainly… well, some time ago, long ago and far away, there were three men who together found a genie's lamp. Being all rather noble and fair-minded and in an exceedingly great hurry to return home, they all agreed that they should rub the lamp together, at one time, and each receive one wish — all of them assuming, of course, that they would be granted the customary three wishes altogether. And, keeping with tradition, the genie confirmed that they could each have one wish only after the mutual awakening.

"Now, it so happened that these three men were all in love with the same woman, a gentle and quiet creature who was very poor. So, the first man wished that the woman he loved would be made a rich princess; and it was done. The second man wished that the woman he loved would always have good health; and it was done. And the third man, he wished that the woman he loved would always find peace and happiness in her life; and it was done.

"Of course, it was only after the men returned home from their travels to find the lamp, that they realized they had all cast their wishes upon the same woman, Joya. Upon learning this, they became insanely jealous of one another and marched straight to the beloved woman to tell her the whole affair that she might choose from among them. But, of course, after hearing their story, she did not know whom to choose! One man had cast her into a fairytale; the other man had given her good health to enjoy it; and the last had cast great peace and happiness over the whole scene. So which man could she choose over the rest?"

"Well, she might have had good health her whole life anyway, and happiness is also a state of mind; but to be made a princess? — *Well, that doesn't happen every day.* She should choose the first man, of course," Ayaz stated, confidently.

"Tsk, tsk," the curtains rebutted. "Are you sure? Good health does not come to all, and what are riches and fairytales if one is suffering from perpetual migraines or fevers? I think the second is worth a great deal of consideration."

"Oh, puffercobs," Ayaz countered.

And on and on they went, debating between themselves the facts of the case before them, each pushing unswervingly for the man of their own choosing until Calah could bear their words no more; after all, didn't she know a thing or two about suitors?

"She should certainly choose the third man! — And that is obvious! For he is the only one who chose for Joya's benefit alone. Wouldn't riches benefit the first man as much as the princess? And wouldn't good health benefit the second as much as Joya too, in that she would never be a burden? But the third man chose something that possibly would not benefit him at all but was wholly for the consideration of Joya's own state of being," Calah said emphatically, though her chin quivered — like knees upon one's first standing — in being moved by her passion.

And the veil — all seven layers — was rent and fell from her face. So, she also removed the veil from her head.

"You have spoken wisely, Princess Calah," Ayaz replied, standing and extending his hand to lift her up from the couch.

She accepted his hand and good Lili danced all the way to inform the sultan of the good news.

Lala Lalu rejoiced when he heard the news and, after the marriage of Ayaz and Calah, he left to retrieve the woodland maiden, as he had promised, with a promise to return to the Golden Valley in due time.

Ayaz sent twenty-four strapping young men from the Golden Valley to the Ruby Village as promised, and Emra sent several cartloads of jewels as many thanks after she and all of her sisters were married off.

The old widow, whose pitchers Ayaz had broken in his youth, was summoned from Wargwherlandia to come and live in the marble castle with Ayaz and Calah.

Osmanek was also summoned for a visit. He saw good Lili's fine manner, and the pair were married the following Spring. Osmanek and Lili were beloved by all in the kingdom and they became godparents to Calah and Ayaz's children.

Ayaz's father had died during his trek and did not live to see these happy days, but a memorial celebration was held for the much-coveted-and-noble pasha in the Golden Valley, and Ayaz made peace with his memories.

The secrets of the nightingale were revealed and treasured. In fact, an entire new garden was made just to honor the dear nightingale who had relieved them all of their fears. And the old widow was most glad to see her old nightingale again, for she was the one who had taught it to speak many years ago. They were inseparable friends again.

But Skeleton Hill was never removed. Like stones stacked upon stones, the bones became a memorial to their children and grandchildren of how much terror can happen when one is careless with their words -

"An injustice of words cannot fix an injustice of heart; they can only cause more injustice," Princess Calah was often heard saying, for she saw and heard and had compassion for others from a whole new perspective now. Stories are still told of her wisdom…

But especially they are told from Ayaz's adoring eyes, who truly loved her from his first thought to find her, to his last breath on earth.